WHALE GETS STUCK!

Whales are some of the most fascinating creatures on earth, and seeing them in the wild is a magical and unforgettable experience! Scientists still don't know why whales perform the great leaps out of the water that got the whale in this story into trouble, but it could be a way of communicating with one another.

Whales face lots of dangers every day, many of them due to the actions of people. Entanglement in fishing nets, captures for marine parks, and pollution in our waters from chemicals, litter and loud underwater noise are just a few of the many dangers that threaten their survival.

WDCS, the Whale and Dolphin Conservation Society, is the global voice for the protection of whales, dolphins and their environment. WDCS is working hard to stop the threats facing whales and dolphins, protect them and the places they live, and to reach out to as many people as possible to help us in our work. To find out more about the work that we do, and the animals that we help, or to adopt your very own whale, visit our website at www.wdcs.org.

For Maddie, Hattie, Ned, Sidney and Eve – KH

For Mum and Dad, Sue Wolfe, Rachel Campbell, Mary Quine and Hugh Norbury – CF

SIMON AND SCHUSTER
This edition first published in Great Britain in 2008
by Simon & Schuster UK Ltd
222 Grays Inn Road, London, WC1X 8HB
A CBS COMPANY
First published in Great Britain in 1993 as
Whale is Stuck by BBC Books.

Text copyright © 2008 Karen Hayles
Illustrations copyright © 2008 Charles Fuge
The right of Karen Hayles and Charles Fuge
to be identified as the author and illustrator of
this work has been asserted by them in accordance with
the Copyright, Designs and Patents Act, 1988
A CIP catalogue record for this book is available from the
British Library upon request
ISBN: 978 1 84738 211 5
Printed in China
10 9 8 7 6 5 4 3

WHALE GETS STUCK!

Charles Fuge & Karen Hayles

SIMON AND SCHUSTER

London New York Sydney

It was midsummer in the Arctic. The sun shone all day and all night, and the sheet of ice that had covered the sea all through the winter was melting and breaking into small islands.

Whale **loved** the open sea.

He **dived** down

into the **deep**,

dark water.

Then he turned, thrust his tail as hard as he could,
and swam back up to the bright surface.

"Look at me!" Whale cried,
as he leapt out of the water.

Fish looked up at Whale and quickly swam aside. He didn't want Whale to land on top of him!

But . . .

SLAP!

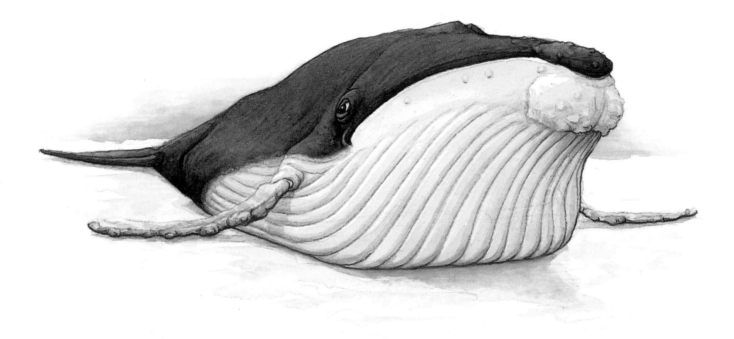

Whale landed right in the middle of an ice floe and, struggle as he might, he was **stuck fast!**

"What am I going to do now?" he spluttered.

Just then, a group of animals arrived to help out. "Don't worry," said Walrus. "We'll soon have you back in the water."

"Dolphins!" he bellowed. "Tip the floe from underneath and I will lever Whale off the ice with my magnificent tusks."

But Whale didn't move an inch!

"I know," Puffin squawked to the birds. "Let's lift him off instead."

The birds flew up and perched on top
of Whale.

"Ouch! Stop!" shrieked Whale as the birds
tried to grip his slippery skin with their sharp claws.
"It won't work," he sighed, sadly. "I'm stuck here forever!"

Everyone gathered around Walrus,
hoping that he would have a bright idea.

Meanwhile, under the water, Fish couldn't see what was
happening up above and he was getting worried.
Why hadn't Whale come back below the water to see him?

By now, a group of polar bears and seals had arrived to see what all the fuss was about.

"That's it!" said Walrus, excitedly. "You seals can help push while I lever Whale with my magnificent tusks and the dolphins tip the ice floe. That should do it!"

So the seals pushed, Walrus strained
and the dolphins tipped, but it was no good –

Whale was still stuck fast!

Poor Whale began to sob quietly.

Suddenly Narwhal appeared. "If Whale leapt *on* to the ice, then he must be able to leap *off* again. Perhaps he just needs a little jab from underneath," he smiled.

He aimed his sharp tusk at the dark shadow above, thrust his tail and …

thump!

Narwhal's tusk wasn't quite long enough.

Whale was still stuck and Narwhal got a nasty bump on the nose.

Meanwhile Walrus had another plan.

"If the polar bears leap onto the edge of the ice and the dolphins tip the other side, then I will lever Whale with my magnificent tusks while the seals push."

So the polar bears leapt, the dolphins tipped,
Walrus strained, and the seals pushed.

The ice floe moved slowly, tipped up,
pointed towards the sky and then . . .

SPLASH!

It fell back into the water and a huge
wave swept everyone clean off the ice.

Everyone, that is, except Whale!

As the day went on, the sun got hotter and brighter, and Whale was **still** stuck. The animals **pushed** and **shoved** until finally they gave up and lay hot and panting on the cool ice.

Deep in the water, Fish peered upwards. And this time he could see exactly what was going on. The heat of the sun and the hot weary animals had begun to melt the ice. Fish could see that the ice was very thin.

Above the surface, the tired animals had not noticed
the creaking and the cracking all around them until . . .

CRUNCH!

All the animals were **plunged** right back into the sea –
including Whale!

Whale was just about to leap out of the water with joy when, "Whale . . . NO!" cried Fish. Whale remembered that his friend was still waiting for him. So, with a slap of his tail, he dived under the water . . .

and the two friends spent the rest of the day
splashing **beneath** the surface together!